For my grandmother, who would have loved this book —JM-M

To Sonny —FB

hmhbooks.com

Illustrations by Fred Blunt
Design by Phil Caminiti
The text was set in Filosofia and hand-lettered.

Library of Congress Cataloging-in-Publication Data is on file.

ISBN: 978-0-358-42333-1

Manufactured in China
SCP 10 9 8 7 6 5 4 3 2 1
4500817410

DON'T SAY

Silly Tongue Twisters to Say
When You Get the Urge

words by **Jimmy Matejek-Morris**

art by **Fred Blunt**

Houghton Mifflin Harcourt

Boston   New York

Let's talk about manners.

There are nice words, like
puppy and buttercup and snickerdoodle,
and there are rude words.

LIKE POOP.

Don't say

It is a very, very rude word.

When you get the urge
to say you-know-what,
try using the much
simpler, sweeter phrase:

Humdrum bum crumbs,

float-or-sinker,

major stinker,

sometimes mushy from your tushy,

smelly belly funky jelly.

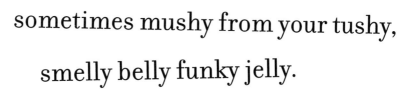

poooo

See how easy peasy push 'n' squeezy?

Never use a word like

That is an absolutely hideous word.

Instead, try:

Dripping zipping

potter squatter,

glitzy spritzy

spray ballet.

Gold-rushing,

bubble-flushing,

sprinkle tinkle liquid trash,

squirting, spurting yellow splash.

Before you let out any humdrum bum crumbs or sprinkle tinkle liquid trash,

be sure to pull down your

polka-dotted,
clean (not spotted),

zip-protector,
hip-collector,

wiseacre
wedgie makers,

and sit on the

flusher gusher
whirlpool chair,

trucking muck to
who-knows-where.

Do you know what a

Burp

or a

Belch

is?

I was afraid you might.

I must insist that instead of saying "I burped," you tell the room that you've been visited by a

sassy gassy,
surprise reprise
misplaced taste.

Now we all know what this is.

Before you shout out that nasty,
nasty word, try calling this a

pant-fitter,

chair-sitter,

gas-spitter,

insulated

tushion cushion.

Don't even get me started on

Everyone knows it's much more polite to say:

Sneezy cheesy
hogger-clogger,
sniffle-snuffle snotter-clotter,
pick 'em, flick 'em,
just-don't-lick-'em
tissue issues.

Worst of all are

Farts.

It is very embarrassing
when these smelly gasses
sneak out through one's

pant-fitter, chair-sitter, gas-spitter,
insulated tushion cushion,

but even more embarrassing
to say or hear such a foul word.

Here we prefer to say:

Butter mutter popcorn boom,
sniff a whiff and clear the room.

Whiny heinie—
wasn't me!

What's that smell?
I have to flee.

Booty tooty, rumble bum,
silent smell phenomenon . . .

. . . earth-shaking,

cheek-quaking,

face reddens,

stench spreadens,

blame-passing,

friend-sassing,

fast-blasting

goof poof.

Excuse me
for that
butter mutter
sputter spoon,
funky, chunky
yellow moon.

Booty tooty
rumble crumb,
polka-dotted
wedgie bum,

sneezy cheesy
push 'n' squeezy,
gooey mooey
whirlpool splash,
tushion cushion
balderdash.

Sniffle snuffle,
wasn't me.

Take a whiff,
now time to flee!

Snickerdoodle,

smelly poodle,

belly grumble,

jelly jumble,

chair-sitter,

pant-splitter,

pick 'em,

flick 'em,

just don't lick 'em,

surprise reprise
goof poof!